Confessions of
an Orange Octopus

CONFESSIONS OF AN ORANGE OCTOPUS

by Jane Sutton

illustrated by Jim Spence

E. P. DUTTON   NEW YORK

Library of Congress Cataloging in Publication Data

Sutton, Jane.
    Confessions of an orange octopus.

    Summary: Nine-year-old Clarence, also known as
Chooch, enlivens a boring summer by teaching himself to
juggle oranges and performing as the Orange Octopus.
    [1. Jugglers and juggling—Fiction.   2. Vacations—
Fiction]   I. Spence, Jim, ill.   II. Title.
PZ7.S96824Co   1983   [Fic]   83-8850
ISBN 0-525-44068-2

Published in the United States by E. P. Dutton, Inc.,
2 Park Avenue, New York, N.Y. 10016

Published simultaneously in Canada by Clarke,
Irwin & Company Limited, Toronto and Vancouver

Editor: Ann Durell   Designer: Claire Counihan

Printed in the U.S.A.   W   First Edition
10 9 8 7 6 5 4 3 2 1

to Poppy
for telling me every week
since I was seven, that I
would be a writer one day

Contents

1

Free at Last

"It's finally here!" said my friend Gary.

"We've been waiting for it since September," said my friend Louise.

"It" was summer vacation.

My friends and I were on our way home on the last day of school. We were really excited about having the summer off. We wouldn't have to go to school or do homework or get up early or wear school clothes for two whole months. We were free!

"My parents want me to go to the school recreation program," I said.

"Yecch," said Louise.

"Double yecch," said Gary.

"Triple yecch!" I said. "I told my parents it was too much like school. And I told them going to school in the fall, winter and spring is plenty."

"Grown-ups don't understand about a lot of things," said Louise.

"That's for sure," I said. "Who else but grown-ups would name a nice little baby who never hurt anyone *Clarence*? It's a good thing you two call me Chooch instead of my real name."

"Do your parents call you Chooch too?" asked Gary.

"No," I said. "They say Chooch is a good name for a dog, not a nine-year-old boy. When I grow up, I think I'll change my name legally to Chooch and get a dog and name him Clarence."

Gary and Louise laughed. I like to make them laugh. The only times I can think of funny things to say is when I'm with people I know well. Mostly when I think of really funny things to say to people, they've just walked out the door.

I've known Gary and Louise forever, because we live in the same neighborhood. That's in Cambridge, Massachusetts, which is famous for having Harvard University in it. Gary and Louise are my two best friends. To tell you the truth, they're just about my only friends. I'm sort of shy with other kids.

We make kind of a funny threesome because we look so different from each other. Louise is very tall for her age. She has blonde hair, wears glasses and is pretty. Gary is short and fat, and he has more freckles than you can count (he tried) and reddish hair. He always wears a Boston Red Sox baseball cap. I'm not fat or skinny, tall or short, and my hair and eyes are dark brown.

The three of us started talking about what we would do over the summer.

2

"I hope I can get my father to take me to a lot of movies and Boston Red Sox games," said Gary. Gary's parents have been divorced for about a year. He lives alone with his father.

Louise said she might visit her friend Alice at her summerhouse in New Hampshire and she planned to do some painting. Louise is a really good artist.

"I'm not sure what I'll do," I said. I wished I had a talent to work on over the summer like Louise. I wasn't crazy about watching movies or baseball games like Gary. I planned to have lots of fun, even if I did nothing. Just not having to go to school would be fun, I figured.

"I have an idea," Louise said all of a sudden. "It seems as if we're always complaining about grown-ups. Why don't we start a gripe club this summer? We could get together and gripe about all the crummy things grown-ups do."

"Sounds like a good idea," said Gary.

I was thinking that Louise always had good ideas. "Let's meet every morning by the slide at the playground," I said.

"This is going to be a great summer!" said Louise.

After a few days of "freedom," my summer didn't seem so "great" anymore. Our Gripe Club meetings were fun. But the rest of the time, I had nothing to do. I must have read all my Fantastic Zippo comic books twice, and I was sick of all my toys and games.

I guess my mother got tired of seeing me moping around the apartment, because she offered to take me shopping one day in July. She had the afternoon off from work—she has a part-time job tutoring kids who are handicapped and can't go to school.

My little brother, Bradford, came on the shopping trip too. Bradford, who went to kindergarten last year, isn't bad for a little brother. I guess I shouldn't complain about being named Clarence. It's better than Bradford.

I took one shopping cart, and my mother and Bradford took another one. I had a great time racing the cart up and down the aisles like a scooter. Pretty soon, my cart was filled. I had an exploding battleship, an air rifle, three Fantastic Zippo comic books and a red robot that walked forward and backward and said "Bcep bop boop."

I met my mother at the checkout line. "All set, Mom," I said.

"Wait a minute, Clarence," she said. "Let me see what you've selected."

The next thing I knew, she had put everything in my shopping cart back on the shelves. She said the air rifle and exploding battleship were too violent. She said the robot would break the first time I played with it. She said I already had enough Fantastic Zippo comic books to last my whole lifetime, and besides, comic books had no culture.

Then she picked out a really boring jigsaw puzzle of the United States and a game that helped you memorize multiplication tables.

"These should keep you busy," she said. "And they're educational."

I didn't bother arguing with her. Grown-ups never understand which toys are decent.

When we got back to our apartment, there was a package from my grandfather, who was on vacation on Cape Cod. It was addressed to me and Bradford.

I knew Gramps would send me something good—he's not your everyday grown-up. Lots of times, he sticks up for me when my parents are mad at me. Sometimes I wish he were my father, instead of my grandfather. Gramps lives just a couple of blocks from our apartment, so I get to see him a lot.

Inside my grandfather's package, there was a yo-yo that glowed in the dark for Bradford and a book called *How To Juggle and Feel Like a King* for me. I was really disappointed. A book about juggling was not my idea of a decent present.

Right away, Bradford started looking through my book, trying to pick out the letters he knows. "There's a *J* and an *F* and a *W*...."

Bradford is really into letters. It gets tiring sometimes. I let him look at the juggling book all he wanted. I didn't care if I ever read it or not.

2

OK, OK, I'll Go

A few days after our shopping trip, my parents got a flyer in the mail telling about a recreation program trip to a natural history museum in Cambridge.

"Why don't you go, Clarence?" my mother asked during dinner. "Maybe it will teach you that there's more to life than TV and comic books."

My mother is really hot on culture. She's always taking courses where they talk about books. I can't understand it. I mean, I like to read all right, but I wouldn't want to sit around and talk a book to death.

"I don't see what you have against the recreation program, Clarence," said my father. "The flyer describes some very interesting activities."

"Well, you can't believe everything you read," I said.

"You're so suspicious," said my father as he reached for a second helping of meat loaf.

"Easy on the meat loaf," said my mother.

My father had a heart attack a couple of years ago. Now he's supposed to stay thin, so he doesn't strain his heart.

He works for a big company that makes medicines. You probably never thought about how medicines look. Well, my father is the guy who designs the boxes and labels and bottles. He decides what color they should be, what kind of pictures to put on the boxes, and things like that.

"Give me one good reason why you don't want to go on the museum trip," my father said to me.

"I feel sick on buses," I said.

"Chew your motion sickness gum," said my mother.

You can't win with grown-ups, I thought. I could have come up with ten good reasons for not going on the trip. And my parents would have found something wrong with all ten of them.

"OK, OK, I'll go," I said. "Maybe I can talk Gary and Louise into going too."

After dinner, I called Louise to ask if she wanted to go on the trip.

"Well, it will probably be yucky," she said. "But I'm getting a little tired of painting all day. So I guess I'll try it."

Then I called Gary. "Sure, why not," he said. "The Red Sox aren't playing that day, and I have nothing else to do."

I'm not the only one having a nothing-to-do-summer, I thought.

As soon as I got on the recreation program bus, I was sorry I had agreed to go on the trip. It was really hot. And it was so crowded that Gary, Louise and I had to sit on the same seat.

Our bus driver must have flunked bus-driving school. If he didn't, he should have. Every time he stopped for a traffic light, the bus lurched forward. And every time he turned a corner, Gary and Louise and I almost ended up in each others' laps.

I think someone sitting behind me brought a salami sandwich for lunch. It really stunk.

We decided to have a Gripe Club meeting.

"I'll start," Louise said, just as the bus driver turned a sharp corner.

I hope I don't puke, I thought.

"The other day," said Louise, "my Uncle Max was talking about the stock market . . . as usual. He had this big mosquito on his nose, and it was all set to bite him. 'Uncle Max,' I said, 'you have a big mosquito on your nose.'

" 'Don't interrupt, Louise,' my mother said.

"Then, when *I* started talking about how me and my friend Barbara saw a wrecking ball knock down a building the day before Barbara left for summer camp, my mother interrupted to say, 'It's Barbara and I, not me and Barbara.' "

Gary and I laughed, because Louise sounded just

8

like her mother. She's really good at imitating people. Louise says funny things all the time, not just in
front of people she knows well. Sometimes she
makes the whole class and even the teacher laugh.

"Hey, man, I have a gripe," said Gary. He once
saw a movie with a character who said "Hey, man,"
and now Gary says it all the time.

"I'm always the wrong age for things," said Gary.
"My father says I'm too young to go see the fireworks
in the park at night by myself. But whenever I do
something dumb, he says I'm old enough to know
better. And whenever I ask him to explain why he
and my mother split up, he says I'm too young to understand."

"I know what you mean about being the wrong
age," said Louise. "I'm supposed to be nice to my little brother because he's younger than I am. I'm supposed to get my father his slippers because he's
older than I am!"

"You can't win with grown-ups," I said. Then I
told *my* gripe. . . . Actually, I had two. First, I told
them about the shopping trip when I got stuck with
the two "educational" toys sitting in the back of my
closet. Then I said, "My family isn't going on vacation this summer because my parents can't afford it.
And the reason they can't afford it is that we're
spending so much money to fly to my Cousin Reggie's wedding in Chicago in August."

"Maybe it will be fun to go to Chicago," said
Louise.

"It won't be fun," I said. "Because my Cousin Reggie's father is my Uncle Andrew. And he's one grown-up you can never win with. When he shakes my hand, he squeezes it so hard that it hurts. And he always shows movies of me when I was a baby, getting my diaper changed. Then he teases me about it."

"Why don't you ask your parents to tell Uncle Andrew not to bug you?" asked Gary.

"It wouldn't do any good," I said. "Grown-ups always stick together."

I was glad when we got to the museum so I could get out of the hot, salami-smelling, lurching bus.

Inside the museum, it was hot too. A skinny woman with greasy-looking hair and thick glasses said she would be our guide and not to touch anything. She looked as if she hadn't smiled in years. In my mind, I named her Miss Grumpy.

She led us to some display cases about American Indians. The cases had models that showed scenes of the Indians in the old days. There were tiny people, tepees, animals, all kinds of cooking equipment, plants, grass and even campfires. I wondered who had built the models. Everything was so small—they looked really hard to make.

Miss Grumpy started talking about the Indians and where they lived and what their customs were. Our group was so big and she talked so softly that I could hardly hear her.

10

"Louder, please!" someone near me shouted. Miss Grumpy talked a little louder for about ten seconds, and then she went back to her soft drone.

After a while, I gave up trying to hear her. I figured I would just look at the display cases on my own. I kind of liked looking at the models and reading the signs. After about the four billionth case, though, I started getting bored. I guess Gary was bored too, because he said, "Hey Chooch, that Indian forgot to put on a blouse."

I looked and sure enough, there was a squaw with her you-know-whats showing.

Gary and I started pointing out all the female Indians that were naked on top. Pretty soon, we were really laughing. Miss Grumpy warned us, "Keep it down back there, or I'll have to ask you to leave the tour."

"Some threat!" I whispered to Gary.

"What are you laughing about?" Louise asked me.

"Young lady, kindly be quiet," Miss Grumpy said.

Gary, Louise and I were quiet for a while. And then I got this funny idea I just had to tell Gary about. "What if the guides here dressed up like the figures in the cases?" I said. "Can't you see Miss Grumpy up there leading us around in nothing but a skirt and beads?"

With that, Gary and I burst out laughing. We couldn't help it. Louise saw us trying to stop laughing and then laughing even harder. That made *her* start laughing too.

Well, I guess Miss Grumpy didn't like the idea of our having so much fun. So she said we would have to leave the group. It was the first time she spoke loudly and clearly.

"Sorry, kids, the rest of you have to stay on the tour," said Louise as we walked away. Everybody started laughing. Except for Miss Grumpy.

One of the recreation program leaders, named Jerry, walked us back to the bus. It was fairly cool inside, because no one else was in it and it was parked in the shade. We sprawled out on three separate seats and ate our lunches.

We decided we would never go on another recreation program trip. Actually, we didn't have much choice. Before he went back to the museum, Jerry told us we had better stay on the bus and wait quietly. And he said if we ever showed up on another trip, he would send us home and call our parents about our rude behavior.

After Jerry stormed off the bus, Gary and Louise and I had a pretty good time. Louise did some great imitations of Jerry and Miss Grumpy. Then we wrote fortunes on slips of paper and put them inside everyone's lunch. We wrote things like *You were just on a boring tour* and *You will soon eat a soggy peanut butter and jelly sandwich.*

It was fun, but I wished I had something else to look forward to over the summer. The only thing that was definitely coming up was my Cousin Reggie's wedding. And I certainly wasn't looking forward to that. I was dreading it.

3

The Night of
The Night Maniac

One rainy afternoon, Gary came over to my apartment to hang out with me. He told me *The Night Maniac* was on TV at nine o'clock that night. He was all excited because he loves scary movies.

"My parents will never let me stay up to watch a nine o'clock movie," I said.

"Tell them it's a great movie, man," said Gary. "Besides, there's no school tomorrow. There's no school for the next six weeks!"

"It won't do any good to try talking them into it," I said. "You know how grown-ups are about sleep. Whenever I want to stay up late, they say I'll be tired and get run down and catch a cold. But when I'm really tired in the morning and don't feel up to making it to school, they say I've slept plenty."

"*I'm* all set for tonight," said Gary. "My father is going out, and the baby-sitter lets me do whatever I feel like. She'll probably let me eat ice cream and popcorn with butter," he said, rubbing his fat stomach.

I wanted to tell Gary to go easy on the ice cream and buttered popcorn. He was too fat as it was. And eating so much didn't seem to make him happy—just fat. But I didn't say anything, because I didn't want to hurt his feelings.

Gary gets away with a lot more stuff than I do since he has only one parent watching what he does. But I wouldn't want my parents to get divorced, no matter how much I gripe about them. And I sure wouldn't want to have to choose which parent I wanted to live with, the way Gary did.

At dinner, I took a chance and asked my parents if I could stay up to watch *The Night Maniac*.

"Absolutely not," said my mother.

"No sir!" said my father. (I *told* you grown-ups always stick together.)

"It's much too violent," said my father.

"It's on much too late," said my mother. "You can stay up for late movies when you're older."

"What's a maniac anyway?" asked Bradford.

"Someone who does crazy things," explained my father.

"Mrs. Matthews does crazy things," said Bradford. (Mrs. Matthews is his baby-sitter.) "The other day, she had on two different color socks."

"Are you leaving your child with a maniac?" I

15

asked my mother with a laugh. Bradford laughed too, even though he probably didn't get it.

"Clarence!" said my father. "That's not funny."

Grown-ups have no sense of humor.

That night, I went to bed at eight o'clock, as usual. But I didn't sleep. I forced myself to stay awake. I almost fell asleep a couple of times, but I made myself think about horrible things—like visiting my Uncle Andrew in two weeks—to keep myself up.

When I heard the TV go on, I tiptoed into the hall. I peeked into the living room and saw my parents sitting on the couch, watching the beginning of *The Night Maniac.* They had a bowl of pretzels on the coffee table in front of them. My father had his arm around my mother.

I had it made! From where I sat in the hall, I could see the TV perfectly. But my parents' backs were toward me. There was no reason for them to turn around because the kitchen and the bathroom—the only places they might go during the movie—were in front of them.

I hoped *The Night Maniac* was as good as Gary said it was.

The movie started out about people camping. It showed all different characters—and some of them were *characters* all right—in a national park.

There was a funny part where a father was loading his station wagon with more and more stuff. Pretty soon, he had to rent a U-Haul trailer at the local gas station. When he brought out an electric frying pan

16

and his wife reminded him there would be no place at the park to plug it in, my father burst out laughing. I didn't think it was *that* funny.

"Shhh! You'll wake Clarence and Bradford," said my mother. *I* almost burst out laughing then.

After the next commercial, the movie wasn't so funny anymore. It started showing this guy with a wild look in his eyes. He kept pulling a knife out of his pocket and sharpening it on a stone. By the time he checked into the national park, you knew some of the campers wouldn't be around by the end of the movie.

My stomach started to feel funny, almost as if I were on the bus on the way to the natural history museum. I would have liked to climb on the couch and sit between my parents. But they wouldn't have been very happy to see me.

The first murder came after the next commercial. It was awful. At least, I think it was awful. I don't know exactly how The Night Maniac killed the girl camper because when he came toward her with his knife, I closed my eyes. I heard a lot of screaming. And if I hadn't had my fist in my mouth, I probably would have screamed too. When I opened my eyes, there was a lot of blood and the tent was all slashed. I wanted to go to bed right then, but something kept me watching the movie. I wondered if Gary was keeping his eyes open during the scary parts.

It got worse and worse. They kept showing The Night Maniac's wild eyes and shiny knife, and the

17

next thing you knew, another camper was dead. I think there were nine people killed by the time the closing credits came on. My mother must have closed her eyes during the scary parts too because I kept hearing her ask, "Is it over yet, Harry?"

At the end of the movie, I felt like asking my parents to tuck me into bed and to check my room to make sure The Night Maniac wasn't in there. But I knew they would be angry if they found out I was up.

I slipped into my room before they could discover me hanging around the hall. I would have liked to keep my light on, but I turned it off so my parents wouldn't suspect anything.

I got into bed. And even though it was a hot night in July, I was shivering. I kept seeing The Night Maniac's eyes. I covered my head with my pillow so he couldn't get me.

After a while, I heard footsteps. They sounded like the footsteps in the movie when The Night Maniac was walking toward a tent. I knew it was just a movie and all. But I lay there terrified just the same. I tried not to move.

Then I heard a voice whispering, "Look, Jan, he's got his pillow over his head." It was my father.

"What a character," my mother answered in a whisper.

Then they left.

I couldn't sleep. Every time I heard a creak in the apartment, I jumped. I must have heard every car, bus and cricket in Cambridge. After a while, the pillow felt too hot, and I took it off. It was then that I saw

19

someone sitting in my rocking chair. It was a man. He smiled at me, and his eyes looked familiar. He had something shiny in his hand. It was The Night Maniac!

I screamed.

The next thing I knew, the light was on, I was sitting up in bed and my mother was hugging me and saying, "Easy, easy, Clarence." I hugged her and started to cry. I was so glad she was my mother and not The Night Maniac.

My father wandered into my room, rubbing his eyes and yawning.

"Were you having a nightmare?" asked my mother.

"Was I!" I said. "I dreamed The Night Maniac was in here. . . . He was going to stab me. . . . It was just like in the movie when . . . uh oh . . ."

"How do you know what happened in the movie?" my mother asked.

"Well, I happened to see parts of it," I mumbled.

"Were you peeking at the movie from the hall, young man?" asked my father.

I couldn't think of a way out. "Yes," I said.

"We specifically told you that you couldn't watch it," said my father.

"Specifically!" said my mother.

"But Gary said it was great!" I said.

"And what did *you* think of it?" asked my mother.

"Not so great," I said. "I sure wish I had gone to sleep instead."

Then my father said that since I had disobeyed, I

would have to stay inside all the next day. I told him I thought my nightmare had been enough punishment. But my mother said they were going to be firm with me to make sure "this kind of thing does not happen again."

When I fell back to sleep, I was lucky enough not to have any more nightmares.

Gary called in the morning and asked why I hadn't met him and Louise at the playground for the Gripe Club meeting. I told him I was grounded for watching the movie.

"I wish you hadn't told me how great it was," I said. "All it did was get me into trouble." I didn't feel like telling him it had scared me so much I had a nightmare.

"Sorry about that, man," said Gary. "What happened at the end anyway? I went to bed after the first murder. It was too scary for me."

Sometimes you can't win with kids either.

4

Grounded

I ended up being stuck in my apartment for four whole days. At the end of the day I was grounded, my throat felt scratchy. By the next morning, my nose was all stuffed up.

My mother said she was sure I had come down with a cold because I had stayed up late to watch *The Night Maniac.* She also said that summer colds are hard to shake and I had better stay inside.

You certainly can't win with grown-ups when it comes to being sick. Let's say you have one little sniffle and you're really looking forward to going to the circus the next day. Your parents say, "You'd better stay home. So much excitement won't be good for you." But let's say you have an awful sore throat and all you feel like eating for dinner is ice cream. Your parents say, "Oh, it doesn't hurt that much. Don't be a baby!"

Anyway, by the second day of being stuck inside, I

was ready to turn into a maniac myself. I had played Go Fish with Bradford three times, and I was sick of it. Besides, it was hard to play cards holding my breath, and my mother kept telling me not to breathe on him. I had also read my library books and all my Fantastic Zippo comic books. It would have been nice if I had some talent or hobby to work on, like Louise has her painting, but I didn't.

After a while, I was so bored that I started reading *How To Juggle and Feel Like a King,* the book my grandfather sent me from Cape Cod. The first part told how much fun it is to juggle and how there have been jugglers all through history. Then it gave instructions.

I got some oranges out of the refrigerator and started the first lesson. All you had to do at first was toss one orange up and down, and then pass it from one hand to the other. There was a special way to throw and catch, even a special way to hold the orange.

Then came the tough part—adding a second orange. You were supposed to remember to wait for the first orange to almost land in your hand before throwing the second one. It was really hard. I kept dropping the oranges, and it wasn't much fun. After a while, I learned to toss them back and forth, from one hand to the other, without dropping them.

When my mother knocked on my door to call me for lunch, I hid the book and the oranges. I wanted to get really good at juggling and then surprise everyone with my hidden talent. It would be neat to have a talent!

I spent the next couple of days in my room with the door shut. I practiced and practiced. My cold was almost gone, but I pretended to keep coughing so that no one would guess that I wanted to stay inside.

After four days, I was ready for three oranges. It was hard at first. But after a while, I was able to juggle three oranges for about two minutes, without dropping any. I could also juggle three tennis balls. I decided I must be one of the people the book called "naturally gifted jugglers." It was the first time I felt naturally gifted at anything. It figured that my grandfather was smart enough to know I would be good at juggling. He knows me better than anyone.

Finally, I decided I was ready to show off. After dinner, I told my parents I wanted them to see something. I asked them and Bradford to sit in the living room. Then I brought out three oranges and juggled all three without dropping one. I even tried a trick I learned from the book, where you throw one of the oranges behind your back every once in a while.

When I was finished, Bradford started applauding wildly. "That was great, Clarence!" he said.

My parents just sat there with their mouths open. It was the first time I had ever left them speechless. I felt like Superboy!

"That was terrific!" my father finally said, clapping along with Bradford.

"Fantastic!" said my mother. "Where did you learn to juggle?"

24

"And when?" asked my father.

I reminded them about the book Gramps had sent me, and I told them I had been practicing in my room for days.

"That shows real self-discipline," said my father.

"It certainly does," said my mother. Suddenly, she slapped herself on the forehead. "Now I know why my oranges disappeared," she said. "After my Great Books class yesterday, I was looking for an orange and I couldn't find any. I just *knew* I had bought three for fifty cents at the A&P. 'Am I going crazy?' I wondered. Then I thought maybe I had accidentally put them in the vegetable bin instead of the fruit bin. So I checked the vegetable bin and . . ."

You can't win with grown-ups. My mother had to go on and on about the oranges—not my juggling. But those few seconds when my parents just sat there with their mouths open made all my practicing worthwhile. Now that I had a talent, I thought my parents might treat me with respect. Maybe *I* would win once in a while.

5

Fame and Fortune, Here I Come

The day after I juggled for my family, the Gripe Club had a meeting. We met at our usual spot—next to the slide at the playground.

"Hey, man, new glasses," Gary said to Louise.

"Don't remind me," she said. "That's my gripe. I *hate* the way I look in these glasses. And my mother says I can't get new ones because I picked these frames out myself. How did I know how terrible they would look after the optician finished them?"

I thought Louise would look good in anything she wore, because she is one of the prettiest girls I know. I didn't say so though. I just said, "You look nice."

"Thanks, Chooch," she said. "But I don't think so."

Gary had a gripe about his grandmother, who had stayed with him and his father over the weekend. He said that whenever he was in the middle of watching a Red Sox game on TV or working on an airplane

27

model, she would say, "Come here and give me a kiss!" And she wouldn't take no for an answer. But when he was hanging around with nothing to do and he asked her to tell him what life was like in the old days or something, she would say, "Can't you find something to do? I'm busy."

I didn't have a gripe. I just said, "I'm kind of hungry." And I pulled an orange out of a paper bag I had and started tossing the orange from one hand to the other.

"I'm *really* hungry," I said. And I took another orange out of the bag and started tossing that one around too.

Pretty soon, I had my three-orange juggling act going, and I had Gary and Louise going crazy. "Wow! *Wow!*" they kept saying. They were jumping up and down. Gary was so excited that he threw his Boston Red Sox cap in the air.

I kept juggling the oranges. It was really neat. I felt like nothing could make me drop an orange. Nothing could hurt me. The oranges floated in the air, making moving patterns.

Suddenly, I noticed a bunch of kids and mothers with babies in strollers watching me. I didn't pay much attention to them because I had to concentrate on my juggling. When I felt my arms getting tired, I caught the oranges one by one and put them down gently without dropping one. There was a big round of applause from the crowd. Without thinking about it, I took a bow.

Before the kids and mothers wandered off, a lot of

them complimented me on my juggling. I actually had a talent!

When my audience left, Gary said, "Hey, man, look at this!" He showed me his baseball cap, which had been lying on the ground after he threw it in the air. There was money in it—people had been putting in money while I was juggling! We counted it up—two dollars and twenty-five cents. It was the first money I had ever earned. And I hadn't even asked for it.

Well, Gary, Louise and I got the same idea at the same time. . . . I could make money juggling! I could buy whatever I wanted with my own money. I had already made two dollars and twenty-five cents in only ten minutes!

The three of us got really excited, thinking I could become famous throughout Cambridge. And rich too. Then we decided that Gary would play juggling music on his kazoo and Louise would introduce me to the crowd and pass the hat. At last we would all have something to do over the summer!

We decided to meet by the playground slide the next day and work on our new juggling act.

I walked home, feeling great about the idea of the act—especially earning my own money. Then I remembered that my grandfather was coming home from Cape Cod that afternoon, and I felt even happier. I spent the rest of the afternoon practicing in my room.

Gramps was invited for dinner that night. I made my parents and Bradford swear that they wouldn't spill the beans about my juggling.

When Gramps showed up, I ran to him and gave him a big hug. He seemed as happy to see me as I was to see him.

"Well, well," he said, looking me over.

He looked great. He had a tan that looked nice next to his white hair. You would never guess from looking at Gramps that he's seventy-five years old. If you heard him talk about the stuff he does, you might think he was about forty. He goes bike riding, and he walks all over the place. Two days a week, he volunteers at an orphanage. He also knows all kinds of card games and card tricks. Gramps isn't shy like me. He seems to know just the right things to say to make friends.

When my father came home from work, we sat around in the living room and my grandfather told us about his vacation. He had gone fishing a couple of times, and he had gone swimming every day, even in the rain. His motel was better than the one he stayed in last year. He said he met lots of nice people, but of course, no one like Bessie.

Bessie was his wife, my grandmother. She died two years ago, and we all miss her a lot. When my grandfather said that about Bessie, my parents and Bradford and I got really quiet. It seemed as if no one knew what to say next.

I had been planning to save my juggling act until

after dinner. But I decided I would do it right then, because Gramps looked as if he could use cheering up.

"I want to show you something, Gramps," I said. And I ran to my room to get oranges.

By the time I had three oranges in the air, my grandfather was on his feet, whistling and clapping. He happens to be a great whistler. My parents and Bradford clapped too. After a while, I added a new trick I had been practicing—I tossed an orange under my leg every once in a while. I didn't drop any either!

When I was finished, my grandfather hugged me and pounded my back with excitement. "You read the book I sent you!" he said. "I knew you could do it!"

I told everybody what had happened on the playground that day.

"What do you know?" said my grandfather. "A real professional juggler with money in the hat!"

I announced that Gary, Louise and I were going to form an act, make all kinds of money and be famous throughout Cambridge by the end of the summer. I was about to ask Gramps what kind of costume he thought I should wear when my father said, "Hold on a minute, young man!"

I could tell there would be trouble because he called me "young man." "What's the matter, Dad?" I asked.

"You are *not* performing for money in public," he said. "I know I don't make that much money, but I won't have my son acting like some . . . some beggar!"

"It's not begging," I said. "I didn't even ask for the money today. People are paying to see me perform."

"No, I don't like it either," said my mother. "You'll run into all kinds of undesirable characters on the streets."

"And when hoodlums see you have money lying around, they'll try to steal it," said my father.

"The money isn't the only reason I want to juggle," I said. "I *like* juggling—I would do it for free."

"No, no, you are *not* to juggle in the streets," said my father. "If I catch you doing it, I will have to take drastic action!"

"Maybe when you're older . . ." said my mother.

"That's what you say about everything," I said.

"You know," my grandfather said softly, "It's really not safe for a child to be out on the street all the time."

I couldn't believe it. Even Gramps was turning against me.

I wanted to tell them all how important the juggling act was to me. But I figured their minds were made up. Also, ever since my father had a heart attack, I try not to make a big fuss about things.

I was angry and sad all through dinner. I didn't know how I would break the news to Gary and Louise the next day.

Then my mother started talking about Reggie's wedding. She reminded my father to get his suit cleaned.

"You should see the nice suit we bought for Clarence!" she said to my grandfather. She smiled at me and said, "Cheer up, Clarence!"

If there was one thing worse than giving up my juggling act, it was the idea of going to that dumb wedding in Chicago and spending time with my Uncle Andrew. And if there was one thing worse than that, it was the idea of wearing a suit.

6

The Birth of Chooch the Orange Octopus

I shouldn't have worried about breaking the news to Gary and Louise. The next day at the playground, Louise told us that her mother had said, "No daughter of mine is going to pass a hat in public." Her father had said, "Don't bother to try and talk us into it, Louise."

Gary's father wouldn't even discuss a juggling act. He had absolutely forbidden Gary to take part in it.

We all felt terrible. "It was a good idea while it lasted," said Gary. He sat on the bottom of the slide, playing with the brim of his baseball cap.

"Now we're back to having nothing to do for the summer," said Louise.

Suddenly, I made up my mind not to be pushed around by grown-ups. I was sick of parents and teachers and recreation program leaders and tour guides telling me what I could and couldn't do. This juggling plan was too good to pass up.

"Well, you two can do what you want," I said. "But I'm going ahead with the act anyway."

"I don't know, man," said Gary. "I'm already in trouble with my father for eating a whole chocolate cake. He was planning to have it for dessert with his new girlfriend. He says I eat too much anyway."

I agreed with Gary's father, but I didn't want to hurt Gary's feelings. So I kept quiet.

"I don't want to get into trouble with my parents either," said Louise. "My mother said next fall she might let me take an art class that my friend Barbara told me about. If she finds out I disobeyed, she'll never let me."

I could understand why my friends didn't want to take a chance. After all, they didn't have as much to gain from my juggling plan as I did. You couldn't get rich and famous from playing a kazoo or passing a hat. But you could from being a juggler.

"Listen," I said. "You don't have to be part of the act. But can you help me think of a name for it?"

"Sure, man," said Gary.

So we started thinking up names. We thought of Chooch the Juggler, The Fantastic Chooch, Oranges and Tennis Balls in Motion, The Flying Fruit Machine and just plain Chooch.

Louise, as usual, came up with a really good idea. She said I could be called Chooch the Orange Octopus. When my hands and the oranges fly really fast, they kind of look like the tentacles of an octopus. Gary and I thought it was a pretty original name. We decided that most likely, no one else in the U.S.A.

had the same name. So it was settled. . . . Instead of dull, shy Clarence Slagovsky, I was someone special —Chooch the Orange Octopus.

Then we planned my costume—an orange T-shirt (which I already had), white shorts (which I already had) and a top hat (which I didn't have). We went to a costume store, pooled our money and bought a top hat.

Our plan was to start the act bright and early the next day. Gary offered to walk me home, and then he asked to borrow my orange T-shirt.

"What for?" I asked. "I need it tomorrow for my costume."

"I'll ask my father to iron it for you," said Gary.

I had never heard of ironing a T-shirt before. But Gary convinced me that it would look much better ironed. He said he felt badly that he wouldn't be playing the kazoo in my act and this was the least he could do for me.

At dinner, my family shared their news of the day. My father told about a new allergy medicine his company was making. He was designing a bottle label for it with a picture of a clock because the medicine was supposed to last twelve hours.

My mother said one of the kids she tutors was going on a long vacation, so she had only two kids to tutor the rest of the summer.

Bradford said that he had seen the letter *Z* three times on license plates that day.

"What's going on with you, Clarence?" asked my father.

I was thinking, *Plenty is new! I'm starting a juggling act tomorrow! And by the way, my name isn't Clarence anymore —It's Chooch the Orange Octopus!* But what I said was, "Oh, nothing much." I couldn't help smiling though.

After dinner, I practiced juggling in my room until I went to bed. Every once in a while, I worried about getting into trouble with my parents for disobeying. But I figured they wouldn't find out about my act right away. And if they found out after I was already a success, they would be too proud of me to be angry.

7

A Brush With the Law

The next morning, I found out that it's not easy to get out of the house carrying a top hat and three oranges in a huge paper bag and wearing white shorts and no shirt (because your friend wanted to iron your T-shirt).

Just as I was about to sneak out the door, my mother spotted me. She said it was too chilly to be going around bare-chested. So I put on a blue T-shirt, figuring I would change later. Then she wanted to know what I had in the paper bag. I wasn't about to tell her I had a top hat and oranges in it, because she would want to know why I needed a top hat and oranges.

"It's just some stuff I need," I said. "I've got to go. Gary's waiting for me."

When we were a couple of blocks from my apartment, Gary pulled my orange T-shirt out of his knapsack. It didn't look any less wrinkled. Then he unfolded it and I saw that across the front, in black letters, it said CHOOCH THE ORANGE OCTOPUS. I didn't mind that at all!

"I had it printed at a T-shirt store near my apartment," said Gary. "Surprised, huh?"

"Yeah, thanks a lot," I said. "It's great."

"Don't mention it, man," said Gary. He looked really pleased. I've heard people say it's more fun to give than to receive, and sometimes I think it's true.

We met Louise at the playground. By then, I was wearing the orange shirt and the top hat.

"Great idea, Gary!" Louise said when she saw my shirt. "You look terrific, Chooch!"

"Where do you want to start juggling?" asked Gary.

"Wait a minute," said Louise. "We haven't even griped yet. . . . Just because Chooch is starting a new act doesn't mean we have to give up the Gripe Club."

"You're right," I said. "I'll start." I told about how I was going to have to wear a suit to that dumb wedding in Chicago, and then I told about how it was hard to sneak out of the house with all my juggling stuff.

Louise offered to keep my oranges and costume at her apartment. She said she could bring them to the playground every morning for me. I thought it was really nice of her. I felt pretty great to have such good friends, and I decided it was better to have two really good friends than ten medium good ones.

Then Louise told her gripe. "When I got home yesterday, there was a picture I painted in school last year hanging in the kitchen. It's really ugly. It was supposed to be mountains and a rainbow, but it looks more like a hamburger and a shake."

Gary and I laughed.

"Well," Louise continued, "I told my mother I didn't want that blob hanging in the kitchen. But she said it was 'very interesting' and I should be proud of it. I decided that having one of my paintings in the kitchen might remind her that I want to take art lessons. So I found another one I like better. It shows a mushroom cloud and dead children and flowers. I wanted it to be a poster against nuclear weapons."

"I remember that picture," I said. "It's really good."

"Well my mother doesn't think so," said Louise. "She took one look at it and said, 'Oh, how violent! Where do you get such ideas?' "

Gary and I laughed, because Louise sounded just like her mother.

"I tried to explain that it had a message," Louise continued. "But she said, 'I will not have that hanging in my kitchen!' "

"Yeah, grown-ups have terrible taste in art," I said. I thought of the dumb-looking picture my parents have in our living room. It's almost all white, with just a couple of stripes on the bottom.

"So what happened to the blob you painted?" Gary asked Louise.

"It's still on the kitchen wall," said Louise with a sigh. "Maybe I'll rip it down in the middle of the night and say that a thief looking for valuable art must have stolen it."

I was getting kind of itchy to get my juggling act started. "Gary, do you have a gripe?" I asked.

"No, man," said Gary. "I feel great today. Let's get this show on the road."

There was a grocery store called Sal's Save-U-More across from the playground. We decided that I should start my act in front of the store, because there were lots of shoppers going in and out. Also, my mother never shops at Sal's. She once bought a package of spoiled chopped meat there, and she never went back.

I took the oranges out of my paper bag, and I put the top hat on the ground in front of me.

"Here, let me put in a dollar," said Gary. "To give people the idea."

I could hardly remember seeing Gary in such a good mood. He moved fast, as if he were much less fat than he was.

I started juggling and soon had all three oranges going. You would think I would be nervous about performing in public. But I wasn't, because I knew I was really good. Also, I remembered what the juggling book said, and I kept my eyes on the oranges and not on the audience.

I heard lots of comments from the shoppers. . . . "Hey, look at that kid!" "What does his shirt say—Chooch the Orange Octopus?" "Hey, that kid's good!" "Look, Mommy, a juggler!"

I also started to hear a ringing sound, and I knew it was the sound of coins hitting each other in my top hat. I wondered what to buy with all the money. I was thinking about getting the robot that said "Beep bop boop," when I heard a siren. It got louder and then stopped.

Suddenly, a voice said, "Hold it right there, son." I jumped, and my oranges splattered all over the sidewalk. Then I saw that the voice belonged to a cop.

I figured my parents had somehow found out about my juggling and had sent a cop to arrest me. My father had warned me that if I went ahead with my juggling plan, he would take "drastic action." He probably meant reform school. I didn't like the idea of being arrested and sent to reform school at all. In fact, I felt like I might puke right in front of Sal's Save-U-More.

"Come with me, son," the cop said. His badge said Officer Simmons. In my mind, I named him Officer Double-chin; you can guess why. He led me to his squad car. The radio was making all kinds of noise and the lights were flashing. I could feel all the shoppers going in and out of the grocery store staring at me. I glanced at Gary and Louise—they looked as scared as I felt.

Officer Double-chin told me to sit in the back of the car and he got in next to me. "Do you have a permit, son? You know, you need a permit from the city of Cambridge to perform in the streets."

Now I knew I was in for it. I had broken a law. "No," I said. "I didn't know about that."

"Well, there's a law that states that not knowing about a law is no excuse," said Officer Double-chin.

"Oh," I said. "I didn't know about that one either." *Reform school, here I come,* I thought.

I was sorry I had ever started juggling. I was sorry my grandfather had ever sent me *How To Juggle and Feel Like a King.* I felt more like a criminal than a king.

"I think I'll run you down to City Hall now," said Officer Double-chin. He got out of the back of the squad car and climbed into the driver's seat.

Gary and Louise came running over to the car. "Don't take our friend away!" said Gary.

"He didn't do anything wrong!" said Louise. I could tell she was nervous, because she kept pushing her glasses back on her nose.

"Your friend has violated a city ordinance," said Officer Double-chin.

I thought Gary and Louise were pretty brave to try and save me from getting arrested. But it didn't do any good. Officer Double-chin sped off. It was just my luck to get into trouble for doing the first thing I was ever good at.

Officer Double-chin drove worse than the bus driver who took us on the recreation program trip. Every time he turned a corner, I practically crashed into the car door. The sun was beating through the windows, and the radio was blaring. I started feeling like puking again. This was not one of the best mornings in my life.

It figured that Officer Double-chin drove like a madman when he was supposed to be setting an example as a good driver. That's the way grown-ups are. Like my father telling me to eat healthy food, snarfing down chocolate-chip cookies two at a time himself. And he's supposed to watch his weight on account of his heart condition.

Officer Double-chin pulled into the City Hall parking lot at about 10,000 miles per hour. Inside City Hall, we walked down a long corridor and stopped at an office that said Licensing Department.

"I have a young man here who's been juggling without a permit," he said to the woman behind the first desk. "May I have a form, please?"

He asked my name and address and birthday, and he wrote it all down on the form. Every time he asked me something, he called me "son." I hate it when grown-ups do that. I'm not his son!

I figured the form would be sent to the reform school principal. I decided I would be really well-behaved in reform school, and then maybe I would only have to stay a couple of months. I decided I would miss Gramps more than anyone.

When Officer Double-chin handed the woman behind the desk the completed form, she said, "That will be five dollars."

"Do you have five dollars, son?" he asked me.

"No sir, I don't," I said. Five dollars didn't seem like too stiff a fine. I hoped it wouldn't be a small fine and then a big sentence in reform school.

"Well, I'll lend you the money for the fee," he said.

And he gave the woman behind the desk a five-dollar bill.

She gave me a little card. I stared at it. . . . It was a permit to perform on the streets in the city of Cambridge. It had my name typed on it, an official City of Cambridge seal, and it said it expired December 31.

"Now you're all set," said Officer Double-chin.

My mouth must have been hanging open about a half mile because he asked, "What's wrong, son?"

"You mean you're not going to arrest me or send me to reform school or anything?" I asked.

Officer Double-chin and the woman behind the desk started laughing. "No, son, is that what you thought?" asked Officer Double-chin. "I just drove you down here to get you a permit." He stroked both his chins and chuckled.

"Thank you, sir," I said, and I remembered how to smile.

Officer Double-chin gave me a ride back to Sal's Save-U-More. He drove like a madman, but I didn't mind this time—I kind of enjoyed the ride. It reminded me of cop shows on TV when the cops chase a criminal. But he was just giving Chooch the Orange Octopus a ride. I laughed to myself.

When we got to Sal's, Officer Double-chin said he would stop by there one day soon so I could pay him back the five dollars he lent me.

"It was very nice of you to let me borrow it, sir," I said.

"That's quite all right, Chooch," he said. "I'll look

forward to catching your juggling act again. You're pretty good!"

I didn't mind him saying that at all! I *felt* pretty good. I even had a permit to perform. Nobody could stop my juggling act now!

8

Nothing Can Stop Me?

Gary and Louise were *very* relieved to see me. They had been hanging around outside Sal's Save-U-More, hoping I would come back.

I told them what happened, and they were really happy about my getting the permit and all. Then Gary told me the good news that I had made a dollar fifty in the few minutes I had been juggling before Officer Double-chin showed up.

Gary said we should use the money to buy oranges to replace the ones that splattered on the sidewalk. "Then you can get back to work," he said.

"Maybe Chooch wants to take the rest of the day off," said Louise. "He must be tired after everything that went on this morning."

"No, I want to get my act going," I said. "I only have a week before I have to leave for that dumb wedding."

We bought enough oranges so we could each eat one for lunch too. Then we sat around talking. Gary went back into the store and bought a couple of candy bars. I wanted to tell him not to eat so much candy. But then I decided I would sound like a grown-up.

When I felt rested, I put my top hat on the sidewalk and started juggling. I must have been looking pretty good because quite a crowd gathered around me, and those coins were ringing in the top hat!

I thought maybe I would have enough money to buy the air rifle *and* the robot that says "Beep bop boop." And then I would buy a new bicycle for Gramps, Boston Red Sox tickets for Gary. . . . I was thinking that maybe *I* could pay for Louise's art lessons, when someone tapped my shoulder. For the second time that day, my oranges splattered all over the sidewalk.

I spun around and saw Sal, the owner of Sal's Save-U-More.

"Excuse me, young man," he said, "but could you move your act somewhere else?"

"Why?" asked Louise, suddenly at my side.

"He's got a permit!" said Gary, on my other side.

"Fine," said Sal. "It's just that you're attracting crowds, and they're blocking the doors. Two customers have complained that they had trouble getting shopping carts out the exit door. And with all the people standing around, the delivery people can't get their trucks close enough to the store."

I didn't like having my juggling act interrupted again. But Sal was being nice, and he did have a point about my audience blocking the doors.

"Do you think you could find another place to juggle?" asked Sal.

"Sure, I guess so," I said.

"I would appreciate it," said Sal. And he went back into the store.

"We can't seem to win," I said. "First we have trouble with our parents, then the police, now Sal. I'll never get my act going."

"We'll just have to find another place for your act," said Gary.

Louise said that the park in front of the library might be a good place to perform. There were always lots of people going to and from the library. We decided to try it.

After we bought more oranges at Sal's, we walked to the park. I felt sure there was no chance that my parents would see me. My father was miles away, at work at the drug manufacturing company, my mother was tutoring a kid who lived on the other side of Cambridge and my grandfather was busy volunteering at the orphanage.

It was possible that a neighbor would see me and tell my parents. But I figured I would be the talk of the town by the time my parents found out.

I put down my top hat and started juggling. Quite a few people stopped to watch and some of them threw money in my hat. I thought that my parents might be so impressed with my earning money that they would let me stay home from Reggie's wedding. I could stay with Gary.

I started thinking how great it would be if I could become as rich as my Uncle Andrew. Uncle Andrew is rich because he's a dentist and he charges his patients lots of money.

Suddenly I heard a loud noise, almost like thunder. The thunder had a voice—it said, "Hey, you!"

I was getting used to having my juggling interrupted, so I was able to catch my oranges one by one instead of dropping them.

The voice of thunder belonged to the most muscular guy I had ever seen. This guy had muscles that looked like mountain ranges. His arms, legs, neck and chest were absolutely bulging with muscles. His head was completely bald. He had a tattoo of a snake on one arm and a tattoo of a pirate on the other arm. He wore shorts like boxers wear and a sleeveless T-shirt that said BIG STU.

Big Stu folded his arms across his huge chest and said, "I want to talk to you."

I was getting sick and tired of grown-ups messing up my juggling act, but Big Stu didn't look like the kind of guy you could pretend wasn't there.

"What do you want to talk about?" I asked him.

"How come you're working my territory?" he asked. "I've been lifting weights right here for years." He pointed to a set of weights under a tree. Next to them was a hat with money in it.

I had never noticed Big Stu in the park before, but I didn't feel like arguing with him. I had a strong feel-

ing that I had come across one of the "undesirable characters" my mother had warned me about.

"There's no room for two street performers here," said Big Stu. "Times are tough. And if people shell out coins for you, they won't feel like parting with any for me.

"One of us will have to move on," said Big Stu. "Which one of us do you think it should be?"

I looked at the muscles bulging in his forearms. I was about to pack up my oranges and leave. But first I tried, "If I juggle on this side of the park and you lift weights by that tree, there would be plenty of room for both of us. Don't you think?" I smiled at him.

Big Stu did not smile back. "Let me put it another way," he said. "If I catch you here again, I'll make you sorry you ever heard of juggling." Then, to make sure I knew he meant business, he poked each word on my T-shirt and said, "Chooch the Orange Octopus." My chest didn't feel too terrific.

"I can take a hint," I said.

Gary, Louise and I must have set a world's record for leaving a park quickly.

My first day as a street performer hadn't worked out at all the way I had planned it.

9

Help!

"You're nuts, man," Gary kept telling me the next morning when we met on the playground.

"I agree with Gary," said Louise. "You're definitely nuts."

"Thanks, FRIENDS," I said.

Gary and Louise thought I was nuts because I was planning to juggle in the park in front of the library in spite of Big Stu's threats. They said Big Stu was no one to fool around with.

I told them I had it all figured out. First, I was going to the police station to give Officer Double-chin the five dollars I owed him. Then I would ask him to talk some sense into Big Stu. When the muscle man saw how friendly I was with a cop, he would be sure to leave me alone.

"I don't know, man," said Gary. "Big Stu could break your legs just by looking at you."

56

Louise agreed to walk to the police station with me. Gary said it was too hot to walk.

"The exercise would be good for you," I said.

"You sound like my father," said Gary. "He's always telling me to stop eating candy and to exercise more."

"Maybe your father is right," I said.

"So now you're siding with grown-ups!" Gary said angrily. "You think you're such a big shot just because you can juggle!"

He started walking away.

"Gary, where are you going?" I shouted after him.

"Away from you—Chooch the Orange Busybody," he said.

"Boy, did I blow it!" I said to Louise. "I really hurt his feelings."

"I'm sure you didn't meant to," said Louise. "Besides, you were right. Maybe you can talk to him later when he cools off."

Then she and I walked to the police station. The policeman behind the main desk said it was Officer Simmons' day off.

"Well, could you give him this tomorrow and tell him it's from Chooch?" I asked, and I handed the policeman a five-dollar bill.

The policeman said he would make sure Officer Simmons got the money and the message.

"What do you want to do now?" asked Louise.

"Go to work," I said.

"Where?" asked Louise.

"At the park in front of the library," I said.

"Without police protection?" asked Louise.

"Big Stu wouldn't do anything to me in public," I said. "He wouldn't want to get arrested."

"There are other places in Cambridge where you can juggle," she said.

"And every one of them has a Sal 'Please Move On' Save-U-More or a Big Stu," I said. "I've got to stop letting grown-ups push me around if I want to get my act going. There are only six days before Reggie's wedding!"

Louise didn't like my plan at all, but she walked with me to the park anyway. I was pulling on my orange T-shirt when I heard her shout, "Chooch—watch out!"

Something hard jabbed my back. "Don't do it, Big Stu!" said Louise.

Big Stu grabbed my shirt and bunched it up over my head so I couldn't see. He shoved the hard whatever-it-was into my back and thundered, "I told you you'd be sorry if I caught you here again!"

"Help!" I shouted. But my voice was muffled inside my T-shirt. "Don't shoot, Big Stu," I pleaded. "Give me another chance!"

I was so scared, my whole body was shaking. I was too young to die—I had a whole juggling career to live for!

"I already gave you a warning," said Big Stu. He dragged me off by my shirt. Louise kept shouting, "Leave him alone!" I could tell she was following us.

I figured Big Stu was leading me to some dark alley to shoot me. If only I had listened to my parents and friends . . .

I heard a sizzling noise, and my back felt wet. Was it blood? Then Big Stu spun me around, and my chest and stomach felt wet too. "That'll teach you, Chooch the Orange Octopus!" he said. He laughed and stomped off.

I was surprised to discover that I was alive.

"You poor thing," said Louise. She helped me pull my T-shirt off. I looked down and saw that my shorts, sneakers, socks, chest, arms and stomach were not covered with blood. They were completely orange.

"I thought he was going to shoot me!" I said to Louise.

"He did," she said, "with a can of orange spray paint."

10

Excuses, Excuses

"I *have* to get this paint off," I said to Louise. I did not want to have to explain to my parents how I happened to become orange.

Louise snuck me into her apartment so I could take a shower. I scrubbed myself with deodorant soap, soap for oily skin, dandruff shampoo and even bathroom cleanser, but the orange paint would not come off. It got a little paler, but it was still there.

"How's it going?" Louise shouted through the bathroom door.

"It's not," I said. "I think it likes me."

"Big Stu's can said 'long-lasting spray paint,' " said Louise.

"Terrific," I said.

Then Louise said I could borrow her brother's long-sleeved shirt and long pants to hide the paint. We figured it was bound to wear off after a while. She opened the door a crack and handed me the clothes. They fit pretty well.

I came out smiling, and I said, "Louise, you're a genius!"

Louise burst out laughing. "You wouldn't think so if you saw yourself," she said. She pointed to my hands, and I saw that they were bright orange.

"Does your brother have any gloves?" I asked.

"You can't wear gloves!" said Louise. She started laughing again. She laughed so hard that she had to take her glasses off and wipe the tears from her eyes. "Don't you think your parents would think it's strange to wear gloves in July?" she asked. "Besides, you'd sweat to death."

"I guess you're right," I said. "But you don't have to laugh so hard. I don't think this is funny at all. How am I going to explain being orange to my parents?"

Just then, the doorbell rang. It was Gary.

"I've been looking all over for you two," he said. "Hey, what happened to you, man?" he asked, staring at my beautiful orange hands.

I didn't feel like explaining being orange to Gary either. So Louise told him all about my meeting with Big Stu. She did a great imitation of Big Stu thundering, "That'll teach you, Chooch the Orange Octopus!"

"I feel terrible," said Gary. "I should have been there to help you."

"That's OK," I said.

"No, it isn't," said Gary. "I feel like a bad friend."

62

"You didn't know Big Stu was going to color me orange," I said. "And listen, I'm sorry I bugged you to get more exercise before."

"In a way, I'm glad you did," said Gary. "I've been thinking about it since I saw you. I don't want to be fat, but I keep on eating. It seems like the more my father yells at me about not eating, the more I eat."

"Did you ever try to stop eating so much?" asked Louise.

"No," said Gary. "I don't know if I can. But I think I'm ready to try. I'm sick of being fat."

"If you really try to eat less, I'm sure you can," I said.

"Do you think you could help me?" asked Gary. "I mean, if you see me buying candy, could you tell me not to? And could you keep reminding me to get more exercise?"

"Sure," I said. I felt pretty great that my talking to Gary had helped him after all. Then I remembered that I was orange. "Speaking of helping somebody, how about helping me think up an excuse for my parents?"

Gary and Louise started coming up with crazy ideas and laughing. Even I started laughing after a while.

Gary said I could hide in his apartment until the paint wore off, and write my parents a postcard saying I was out of town on a secret mission. Or I could tell my parents that being orange was a new fad.

Louise suggested that I just keep saying, "Me? Orange? I don't know what you're talking about!"

Then she said I could say I fell into an orange paint puddle.

I knew there was no excuse my parents would believe—I would have to tell them the truth. And I wasn't looking forward to it at all.

Gary tried to cheer me up. "Maybe you'll get out of going to your cousin's wedding," he said. "You can't go to a wedding orange!"

11

Punishment Time Again

Turpentine. Now why hadn't I thought of that?

Turpentine is what my father used to get the orange paint off me. I didn't smell too good afterwards, but at least I wasn't orange anymore.

Disappointed. That was the word I kept hearing after I told my parents how I happened to become orange. My mother was disappointed that I had disobeyed them about my juggling act. My father was disappointed that I hadn't confided in them that I had been threatened. Even my grandfather said he was disappointed that I "hadn't shown better judgment."

It seems to me that grown-ups say they're disappointed when they're just plain mad at you.

Punishment. After my parents stopped carrying on about how disappointed they were in me, they discussed what my punishment should be. I suggested that they make me stay home from Reggie's wedding, but my father just gave me a dirty look.

My mother suggested that I be made to stay in the house for a few days as a punishment. But my father reminded her that they had already used that one after *The Night Maniac* incident and it hadn't made much of an impression on me.

"How about no TV for a week?" my father said.

"That's not fair to Bradford," said my mother. "We would have to leave the TV off, and Bradford couldn't watch either."

Then Bradford piped up, "I don't think Clarence needs a punishment. Big Stu already punished him." I *told* you Bradford's not bad for a little brother.

My parents ignored Bradford's suggestion.

My grandfather commented that my punishment should be useful somehow. He said, "I read in the paper that instead of wasting the taxpayers' money on jails, judges are putting lawbreakers to work doing useful jobs. . . . How about if Clarence volunteers with me at the orphanage once a week for . . . let's say . . . two months?"

"Sounds like a good idea," said my mother.

"Yes," said my father. "Not only will he be doing something useful, but he will be safe in the orphanage. We won't have to worry about him getting spray-painted by muscle men."

"What do you think, Clarence?" asked my grandfather.

I supposed it was better than being stuck inside for a week, or not being allowed to watch TV, or having my Fantastic Zippo comic books taken away (my parents tried that one last year when I hid a puppy in my room for two days and the puppy wasn't toilet-trained).

Volunteering at the orphanage also meant I would get to be with Gramps a lot. But I didn't like the idea of all those kids. I've baby-sat for Bradford a couple of times, and I've gotten pretty bored after about ten minutes. In the orphanage, there would be a hundred Bradfords! And some of the kids would be my age or older. It's hard enough for me to talk to the kids in my school. What would I say to a bunch of orphans I had never seen before?

But I figured that the grown-ups wouldn't listen to my worries about the orphanage plan anyway. So I said, "It sounds fair to me."

It was settled. I would start volunteering at the orphanage the next week . . . after we got back from (groan) the wedding.

12

Meet Uncle Andrew

"Have a wonderful trip!" said my grandfather when he dropped us off at the airport. He was in a great mood. Why not? *He* didn't have to go to the wedding. He's my father's father. And Uncle Andrew is my mother's brother. So Gramps isn't related to anyone in the wedding. He's got all the luck.

My father gave me some special gum with medicine that's supposed to prevent airsickness. He thinks it's great because it's made by the company he works for. All it really does is make you sleepy. It didn't stop me from feeling sick, but I was too sleepy to puke.

Even if I hadn't been on a plane, I think I would have felt sick about the idea of seeing Uncle Andrew, Aunt Myrna and my Cousin Reggie. I kept thinking that grown-ups have the worst taste in people. My mother actually *likes* her brother Andrew! She thinks he has a great sense of humor. And she thinks Aunt Myrna is "sweet" and Reggie is "darling." Teachers always have bad taste in people too. The best kids are always getting into trouble for being fresh. And the creeps are the teachers' pets.

When Uncle Andrew spotted us walking through the gate at the Chicago airport, he smiled and waved and whooped. He was so loud that everyone around him stared at him. He even looks loud—he has a bright red face and thinning, red hair, and he wears loud clothes. That day, he had on plaid pants and a purple shirt. I'm surprised we didn't see him while we were still in the air.

I would have liked to walk right past Uncle Andrew and pretend I didn't know him. But he ran up to us and gave my parents big hugs. Then, as usual, he shook my hand so hard that it hurt. "How you doing, sport?" he asked.

I was thinking, *Fine, until you squeezed my hand to death.* But I just said, "Fine, thanks." I never let on to Uncle Andrew that his handshake hurt. I wouldn't give him the satisfaction.

Then he shook Bradford's hand. "Ow!" said Bradford.

"Ha ha, that didn't really hurt, did it Braddy?" said Uncle Andrew.

After we picked up our luggage, Uncle Andrew led us to the parking lot, where he had a new Lincoln Continental. I knew he would bore us to death all the way to his house about what a great car it was, and I

was right. Uncle Andrew thinks everything he does and has is the greatest. I had never heard him admit that he was wrong about anything.

After he finished boring us about the car, he bored us about how he had hired the best band in the Chicago area to play at Reggie's wedding the next day. And the food and the flowers and the hotel for the wedding reception were all the best in Chicago too. Even the tuxedos he and Reggie were going to wear were the best, according to Uncle Andrew. And so was the minister!

Bradford was smart—he fell asleep in the car. I was too hungry to sleep. I hadn't eaten any of the horrible food on the plane. And after the airsickness medicine gum wore off, I was starving.

When we got to Uncle Andrew's house in Wheaton, which is a suburb of Chicago, I remembered why I'm not crazy about Aunt Myrna. Maybe my mother thinks Aunt Myrna's sweet, but I think she's just plain annoying. She has an annoying squeak of a noise that's as quiet as Uncle Andrew's is loud. And she's always saying things like "Aren't you the young man now?"

Uncle Andrew and my father unloaded the car, and my mother, Bradford and I went into the house. It's huge. You could fit our apartment into it four times.

"Aren't you the young man now?" Aunt Myrna squeaked when she saw me. Then she put her cheek against my lips, so I had to kiss her or be rude.

Reggie came downstairs. He is Uncle Andrew's

and Aunt Myrna's only child. They think he's the best son in the Chicago area. Just about every week, Uncle Andrew sends us a newspaper clipping about Reggie. The clippings have headlines like: "Local Boy Wins Swim Meet" or "Reggie Henderson Elected Class President at Princeton University." This summer, there was one that said "Princeton Graduates Wheaton Man With Honors."

My parents are always impressed with the newspaper clippings. They probably wish they had a son who would get his name in the paper. I've never done anything special enough to get into the paper. Now that there is something special about me—I can juggle—they won't let me do it in public.

Reggie is an excellent student, an excellent athlete and excellent looking. But you can tell *he* thinks he's the best son in the Chicago area too, or maybe in the whole U.S.A. He's the kind of person who asks you a question and doesn't listen to your answer. I felt sorry for the girl he was marrying the next day. I heard her name was Pam and she was from Wheaton too.

"Reggie, are you nervous about the big day tomorrow?" my father asked Reggie.

"No no, not me," said Reggie with an aren't-I-handsome smile.

After what seemed like hours and I thought I would faint from hunger, Aunt Myrna served us lunch. "Aren't you a good eater?" she kept saying to me as I polished off three egg salad sandwiches. I don't even like egg salad.

"What grade are you in, Clarence?" Reggie asked.

I was about to tell him I would be in fifth grade in the fall when Reggie asked, "Could you pass the potato chips, Mother?"

After lunch, Uncle Andrew said we *had* to go to this wonderful country club they had joined.

Now he'll say it's the best country club in the Chicago area, I thought.

"It's the best country club in the Chicago area," said Uncle Andrew.

The last thing I felt like doing after riding in a plane from Boston to Chicago and then riding in a car from the airport to Wheaton was get back in the car and ride some more. But I knew I couldn't get out of going. My parents kept saying how "refreshing" it would be to go for a swim.

When we got to the country club, Uncle Andrew asked six people to move out of their lounge chairs so that our group could sit together. He had on a yellow and turquoise bathing suit as loud as his voice.

Reggie took off his shirt right away and plunged into the pool. He had a nice tan and lots of muscles.

"Look at that swimming stroke!" said Andrew, pointing at Reggie. "Three times, he won the fifty-yard swim meet at Princeton. Three times!"

The country club was pretty, I had to admit. The pool was shaped like a peanut, and there were willow trees all around it. There were even waiters who served you drinks by the pool. The lounge chairs were really comfortable. I lay back in mine and closed my eyes. There was a nice, cool breeze.

73

"Well, I think I'll hit the pool," announced Uncle Andrew.

"Me too," squeaked Aunt Myrna.

"Me too, me too!" said Bradford. My parents said they would take him in the shallow end.

I was lying on my lounge chair, relaxing, when something freezing touched my shoulder. I jumped. It was the dripping wet hand of Uncle Andrew. "What's the matter, sport, don't you know how to swim?" he bellowed.

"Sure, I know how to swim," I said. "I just don't feel like it right now."

"Aah, you probably can't swim," he said. Grownups are always saying that they bet you can't do something when they want you to do it. I wasn't about to fall for that old trick.

Then my parents showed up. "Clarence, aren't you going in the water?" asked my mother.

"Uncle Andrew was nice enough to bring us here as his guests," said my father. "Aren't you going in?"

"Naah," I said. "I want to rest for a while."

"The swim will do you good after the plane ride," said my mother.

"OK, OK, I'll go in," I said. The lounge chair wasn't so comfortable now that everyone was bugging me.

It turned out that there were some really neat Styrofoam kickboards in the pool. I had fun motoring up and down the pool with a kickboard in front of me and then diving under it. Then I joined Bradford at the shallow end, and we had races. We made a rule that he had to swim half a length for each full length I swam.

After that, we played a game where I jumped into the pool and swam underwater to where Bradford was standing. We were both enjoying the game a lot when we heard, "Boys, you've been in the water long enough!"

"Oh, Mom, this is fun," said Bradford.

"I knew the kids would love it here," said Uncle Andrew.

"Come out of the water right now!" said my mother. "Your lips are turning blue."

You can't win with grown-ups. They bug you to get in the water when you don't feel like it. Then just when you're starting to enjoy it, they say your lips are blue.

When we came out of the water, Aunt Myrna said, "Aren't you young men the swimmers?"

Uncle Andrew said, "You should have seen Reggie when he was Clarence's age—he was already winning swim meets!"

Reggie lay in the sun, smiling an aren't-I-something smile.

I lay in the sun too. It felt nice and warm after swimming.

"Don't get too used to this, sport," Uncle Andrew said to me. "You won't want to go home."

I didn't like Uncle Andrew saying that at all. I thought it would make my father feel bad that we didn't have enough money to join a country club. We had spent all our recreation money just to fly to Chicago for Reggie's dumb wedding. I didn't want my father to worry about money and have another heart attack. I thought I would much rather have him for my father than rich, loud Uncle Andrew.

That night, we all went out to dinner with Pam, Reggie's fiancée, and her family. We went to The Blue Table, which Uncle Andrew said was the best restaurant in Chicago.

My father ordered chopped sirloin (that's a fancy name for hamburger) for me and Bradford. The meat was practically raw on the inside. I just ate the outside edges. If you ask me, McDonald's makes better hamburgers than The Blue Table.

Pam and her family were pretty nice. And Pam was beautiful. I don't know why she was marrying Reggie. I wanted to talk to her, but since I didn't know her, I couldn't think of anything to say.

I missed my friends back home. If Gary and Louise were with me, we would have found plenty to gripe about. And Louise could have done a great imitation of Uncle Andrew.

After dinner, we went back to Uncle Andrew's and Aunt Myrna's. Naturally, Uncle Andrew herded us into his family room and showed movies of visits when Bradford and I were babies.

I tried to get out of the room before the part with me getting my diaper changed. Just as I got up to leave, Uncle Andrew said, "Don't leave now, sport. Here comes the best part!" And then everyone laughed to see me lying on my back, kicking my legs, with a grin on my face and wearing nothing but a

shirt. I felt even more embarrassed than usual because Pam was there.

Grown-ups like Uncle Andrew sure know how to make you feel awful. I thought of asking my parents to tell him not to show that movie anymore and not to squeeze my hand until it hurt and not to call me "sport." But I figured they would never take my side against a grown-up.

13

The Wedding

When I woke up at seven o'clock in the morning, Uncle Andrew was already dressed for the wedding. With his red face, red hair and a *green* tuxedo (that's right—green), he looked like Christmas in August. I wondered if his dentist uniform was pink or purple instead of white.

I finished breakfast quickly and then went to my room to practice juggling with some tennis balls I had packed. I waited until the last possible minute to put on my suit. My mother tied my necktie for me. I sure hate ties. I felt as if I couldn't turn my neck.

Outside the church, there was a whole bunch of relatives I hardly knew. My mother kept telling me to kiss them. Grown-ups are always telling you not to talk to strangers—even if they offer you candy or a ride home or money. And here I had to *kiss* all these people who were practically strangers.

A lot of them asked my parents how old Bradford and I were, as if we couldn't speak English. When my mother would say, "Five and nine," the relative would say, "Aren't you big boys?" or "Haven't you grown?"

After a while, I felt like saying, "Congratulations! You've just won a prize for being the ten thousandth person to have said the same thing!" But I just kept smiling.

The wedding ceremony took ages. If I ever get married, I'll just have the minister say, "So, you two want to get married? I now pronounce you husband and wife." I would leave out the kissing part.

When the ceremony was finally over, there was a receiving line. You were supposed to stand in line and wait your turn to shake hands with the people in the wedding. When I got to Uncle Andrew, he squeezed my hand so hard, I thought it would shrivel up. But I didn't say anything.

Pam gave me a pretty smile when I shook her hand. She looked beautiful in her wedding gown. I still couldn't figure out why she was marrying Reggie. Uncle Andrew probably told her Reggie was the best catch in the Chicago area or that he would torture her with his dentist's drill if she didn't marry him.

When everyone got through congratulating everyone, we drove to a big hotel for the reception. I asked my parents if I could take off my tie, now that the church part of the wedding was over.

"Certainly not," said my mother.

"Of course not," said my father.

Didn't I tell you grown-ups always stick together?

My mother reminded me that I was a guest and I should behave. According to grown-ups, you always have to be nice when you're a visitor. Then when someone visits *you,* you have to be nice because you're the host. Sometimes I get sick of being nice—it usually means doing things someone else's way and not how I want to.

At the hotel reception, there were so many waiters and waitresses running around with trays of appetizers, they looked like ants. I had to admit that the appetizers (which Uncle Andrew said were from the best caterer in Chicago) were pretty good. I really liked the tiny hot dogs and egg rolls. Gary would have gone crazy over them!

But the band, which Uncle Andrew said was the best in the Chicago area, was TERRIBLE. It was called Jack and the Moonlighters. Jack talked into the microphone a lot, played the accordion and sang off-key. The Moonlighters, who were about as talented (or untalented) as Jack, were two guitar players and a drummer.

Jack announced that the newlyweds would dance the first dance. Everyone applauded while Reggie and Pam whirled around to some corny song. Naturally, Reggie was an excellent dancer. He had probably won 16,000 dance contests at Princeton.

After that, Jack invited Reggie to dance with Aunt Myrna, and everyone applauded. Then Pam danced with her father, and everyone applauded. It was really boring.

When the band took a break, everyone sat at round tables with flowers in the middle. The ant waitresses brought out cups of soup. Bradford gave me his, because he hates soup.

While we were eating, the band started to play again and Jack invited Uncle Andrew and Aunt Myrna to get out on the dance floor. You should have seen Uncle Andrew strutting around in his green tuxedo. He really showed off—he twirled Aunt Myrna in so many circles that she must have felt like puking up the soup and tiny hot dogs. Everyone applauded. Not me.

The meal took forever. They dragged it out so people could dance between courses.

After Reggie and Pam cut the wedding cake and everyone had a piece, I thought we would finally be leaving. Just then, Jack announced, "And now we'll dance the afternoon away." He started to play a song called "Night and Day." My parents headed for the dance floor with real mushy expressions on their faces.

Now we'll never get out of here, I thought.

I was about to ask Bradford if he wanted to play Twenty Questions, when something strange happened—the music stopped. I looked at the band platform—Jack's mouth was moving and the Moonlighters' hands were moving on their instruments. But there was no sound except for the drum. Then the drum stopped too.

A green flash headed for the band platform. It was Uncle Andrew. He tried to fix the microphone. Jack and the Moonlighters fiddled around with the wires connected to their instruments. There was still no sound.

All the dancers went back to the round tables with flowers in the middle. Uncle Andrew started waving his arms and stamping his feet. His red face was redder than ever.

"Why is Uncle Andrew dancing all by himself without any music?" asked Bradford.

"He's not dancing, honey," said my mother. "He's just blowing off steam."

I burst out laughing. The sound system for the "best band in the Chicago area" at the "best hotel in Chicago" had just plain died.

"It's not funny, Clarence," said my father.

I *told* you grown-ups have no sense of humor.

Uncle Andrew didn't need a microphone to be heard. "We'll fix it in a minute!" he shouted. Then he disappeared and came back with some hotel employees and a new microphone. They connected it, but nothing happened. Uncle Andrew paced the floor next to the band platform, waving his arms.

The ant waitresses brought a bowl of fruit and a bowl of mints to each table.

"What a shame that the sound system failed," said my mother.

"Poor Andrew," said my father.

I tried not to start laughing again. It was the first time I had ever seen Uncle Andrew look embarrassed. He had made such a big deal about how great his son's wedding would be, and now there was no music.

"Anyone know how to tap dance?" he shouted with a nervous laugh. "We need some entertainment."

I looked at the bowl of fruit on our table, and I looked at Uncle Andrew. I took an orange and started tossing it from one hand to the other.

My mother caught my eye. She guessed what I was thinking, and we smiled at each other. "Go ahead," she said.

"Can I take off my jacket and tie?" I asked.

"Sure," she said.

My mother and I borrowed oranges from other tables' fruit bowls, and we headed for the band platform. By then, Jack and the Moonlighters had disappeared.

"I'll murder them!" Uncle Andrew was muttering. "They can't do this to me."

"Andrew," said my mother, "we have some entertainment to take the band's place."

"Really?" asked Uncle Andrew.

"Clarence happens to be an excellent juggler," said my mother.

"Come on," said Uncle Andrew. "People are laughing at me enough without the kid making a fool of me *and* himself."

"I'm telling you—he's very talented," my mother said firmly.

"Sure, sure," said Uncle Andrew. "Oh, what have I got to lose? Go ahead. . . ." He made his hands into a megaphone and shouted, "And now, my nephew, Clarence Slagovsky, from Cambridge, Massachusetts, will entertain you."

He and my mother went back to their seats. This was the biggest crowd I had ever performed in front of. There must have been 300 people out there.

I got two oranges in the air and immediately dropped one. I started again, but my fingers slipped, and I dropped an orange again when I got up to three.

All those tiny egg rolls and hot dogs were rumbling around in my stomach, and I started to feel sick. I could feel people staring at me, probably trying not to laugh. Out of the corner of my eye, I saw a green splotch—Uncle Andrew. He was right—I was making a fool of myself. I started again and dropped another orange.

I was about to go back to my seat when my mother ran up to the band platform. "Take a deep breath," she said. "I know you can do it."

I took a deep breath. And I moved my shoulders around to loosen them up. "There are so many people, Mom," I whispered.

"Bradford asked me to give you a message," said my mother. "He said, 'Tell him to do that neat move when he throws an orange behind his back.' "

I had to smile at that. Then I got an idea. I tried to forget about all the people out there. I pretended I was juggling in front of Gary and Louise and a few of Sal's Save-U-More customers.

I tossed an orange into the air, then two, then three. I was doing it! I kept the oranges moving, nice and smooth. Everyone started clapping, which reminded me again that there were about 300 people out there.

I started getting nervous again. But I got a hold of myself and didn't drop any oranges. I thought how surprised Uncle Andrew must be to see I could really move those oranges around. I smiled to myself, and then the juggling started to go easily.

I did my behind-the-back move especially for Bradford. Then I tried some new moves I had been practicing in secret. I grabbed a fourth orange. It worked! I was actually juggling four oranges!

Soon everyone was standing up and applauding. When I felt I had performed enough, I caught three oranges, spun around as I caught the fourth and took a bow.

Uncle Andrew ran up to the band platform and shouted, "Let's hear it for my nephew, Clarence! He's the best juggler east of the Mississippi!"

He hugged me and said, "I was wrong about you, sport. You saved the day!"

I never thought I would hear Uncle Andrew admit he was wrong about anything! Hearing him say I had saved the day and getting 300 people to stand up and cheer made going to Reggie's dumb wedding and even wearing a suit and tie all day seem worthwhile.

14

Home Again

The day after the wedding, I was back in Cambridge, and Gary, Louise and I met by the slide in the playground. I decided to let them tell their news first. I wanted to save telling about my juggling at the wedding the same way I save my French fries to eat after my hamburger and peas. That way, I have something to look forward to.

Gary and Louise had great news too. Gary hadn't eaten one piece of candy the whole weekend I was in Chicago, and he had actually turned down dessert twice! Louise had had a great time at her friend Alice's summerhouse in New Hampshire. And when she got home, her mother told her she could take art lessons in the fall.

Then it was my turn. Gary and Louise laughed their heads off when I told them about Uncle Andrew ranting and raving and huffing and puffing about the sound system in the best hotel in Chicago. And they thought it was super that I had performed in front of everyone at the wedding and that I could juggle four oranges.

"You know what?" said Louise. "This is the first time this summer that we've gotten together without griping!"

That afternoon, I went with Gramps to volunteer at the orphanage. He took me to a little courtyard where the kids play. Right away, about ten little kids came over to Gramps and hugged him and kissed him.

One little girl started holding my hand. She must have been about three. She kept looking up at me and smiling. I felt really sorry for her because she was an orphan. I wished I could do something for her. All I could think of was to say "Hi."

"This is Tina," said my grandfather.

"Hi," I said again. I felt like a dope.

My grandfather was great with the kids. He fooled around with them and admired the drawings they showed him.

Then some kids who were my age and older came over to greet my grandfather. I could hardly look at them—I felt so guilty that they had no parents and I had such nice ones. They slept ten to a room, and I had a room of my own. I promised myself that I would never gripe about my parents again, or at least not so often.

I'm too shy to be a volunteer, I thought. I was no help

at all. I kept standing around feeling sorry for the kids and not knowing what to say except "Hi."

But Gramps knew just what to say. "Everybody, sit down in a circle," he said. "Come on, Jeff. . . . You too, Sally."

When the kids were seated, he said, "We are lucky today to have a talented juggler with us. . . . He has performed in Cambridge and Chicago. And here he is—Chooch the Orange Octopus."

He pointed to me, and the kids clapped. Then he pulled four tennis balls out of his jacket pockets and handed them to me.

I was really happy to have something to do for the kids. And I didn't have to think of a word to say.

I started juggling, and the kids loved it. They oohed and ahhed and cheered and clapped. When I was finished, they yelled, "More! More!" So I kept juggling until my hands got too tired.

A bunch of kids came over to me with pencils and little pieces of paper. They wanted my autograph! No one had ever asked me for my autograph before. I signed about twelve pieces of paper: *To* (whatever the kid's name was) *Best wishes, Chooch the Orange Octopus.* I thought maybe I would become famous throughout Cambridge after all.

After that, I didn't feel shy around the kids. Tina and a couple of her friends took me on a tour of the orphanage and we played tag in the courtyard. Gramps showed some of the kids card tricks.

I was in the middle of a game of tag when Gramps said it was time for us to leave. All the kids groaned.

"We will be back next week," he said.

"Chooch too?" asked Tina.

"I'll be here!" I said.

I decided I liked helping at the orphanage after all.

"It's too bad you can't make money being a volunteer," I said to my grandfather as we walked home.

He laughed. "You'd like to earn some money, would you?" he asked.

"I sure would," I said. "Then I could buy whatever I want, without grown-ups telling me what I can or can't have all the time."

"I have a plan that might help you make money," he said.

"What plan?" I asked. "Tell me!"

"I have to give it more thought," he said.

"Give me a hint," I begged.

"I'm coming to your place for dinner tonight," he said. "Can you wait until then to talk about it?"

"No," I said. But I did.

15

The Plan Is Revealed

Gramps waited until dessert to talk about his plan. I thought I would die of curiosity all through the spaghetti and salad. I hoped that I hadn't inherited my father's heart condition, because I thought the suspense might give me a heart attack.

My grandfather talked about Cape Cod, the orphanage, the cost of heating oil—everything BUT the plan.

Finally, he said he had gotten an idea when he heard about my performance at Reggie's wedding. His plan was for me to entertain at parties. I could advertise in the paper and get jobs after school and on weekends, at children's birthday and holiday parties.

"I don't know," said my mother. "He would be going into the homes of strangers."

"I don't know either," said my father. "I wouldn't

want Clarence traveling all over Cambridge by himself."

You can't win with grown-ups, I thought. Here my grandfather had come up with a terrific plan, and my parents had to find all kinds of things wrong with it.

"Maybe he can try it when he's older," said my mother.

"Nine years old is kind of young to be in business for yourself," said my father.

I was so angry and sad and every other bad feeling you can think of that I couldn't sit at the dinner table anymore. So I ran to my room and closed the door. I threw myself on my bed and cried into my pillow so no one would hear me.

It wasn't fair! I finally had a talent and what good did it do me?

After a while, there was a knock on my door. "Who is it?" I asked.

"It's Mom and me," said my father.

I wiped my eyes and pretended to be reading a comic book. "Come in," I said. I figured I was in for a lecture about how some things have to wait until you're older and about comic books not having any culture.

When they walked in, my parents had big smiles on their faces. My father sat in my rocking chair, and my mother sat on my bed.

"We did some talking before your grandfather went home," said my mother. "And we came up with a new plan!" Then she told me I could perform at

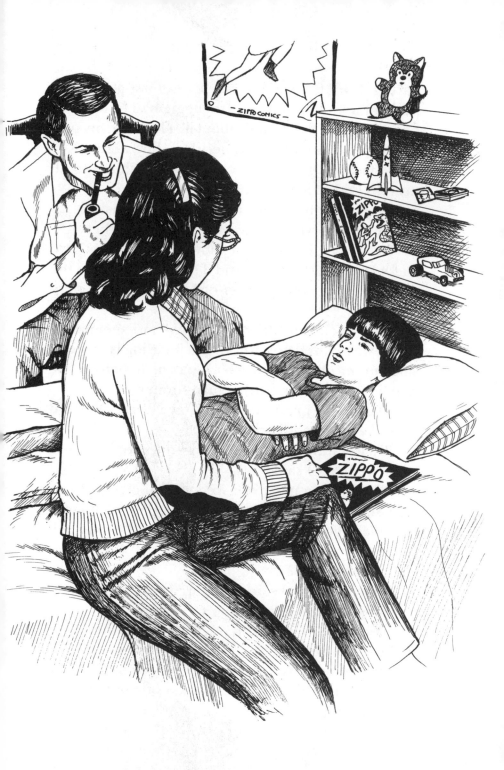

parties . . . *if* I followed certain rules. First of all, people who wanted to hire me to juggle had to come to our apartment first to talk about it. That way, my parents could meet them and decide if they were OK.

Second, my grandfather would go with me to all my jobs and walk me home.

"Gramps wouldn't mind doing that?" I asked.

"He said he would enjoy it," said my mother.

"He said he might even show the kids a few card tricks," said my father. "And if he's ever busy on the day of a party, your mother or I will go with you instead."

"When you ran off from dinner and seemed so upset, we realized how important juggling is to you," said my mother. "If we had known it before, we might have come up with a plan sooner."

"I think it's a great plan," said my father. "You did so well at the wedding!"

"Uncle Andrew didn't even squeeze my hand when we left," I said.

"What do you mean?" asked my father.

"Oh, he used to shake my hand so hard, I thought I'd have to go to the Emergency Room," I explained.

"That's terrible," said my mother. "Why didn't you tell us before?"

"I don't know," I said. "I figured you wouldn't do anything about it because he's a grown-up."

"Of course we would have," said my father. "No one should get away with hurting someone. We'll talk to him about it the next time we see him."

"While you're at it, would you ask him not to show

96

the movie of me getting my diaper changed?" I asked.

"Sure," said my mother. "You never let on that it bothered you."

"You should tell us how you feel about things," said my father.

"Well, maybe I will from now on," I said.

"There's still one thing that bothers me about your juggling," said my mother. "Couldn't you call yourself *Clarence* the Orange Octopus?"

"Chooch is a lot catchier," I said.

"Well, OK, it's *your* act," said my mother.

Sometimes you CAN win with grown-ups, I thought.

Epilogue: A Professional!

When Gary and Louise heard about my new juggling plan, they offered to help spread the word. Louise made some really nice posters. And she and Gary hung them on bulletin boards at the library and Sal's Save-U-More and other places in the neighborhood.

The very day that my friends put up posters, I got three calls. One man said he would keep me in mind for a Christmas party he was planning. One lady said my rate, ten dollars a party, was more than she wanted to spend. And one lady asked if I could entertain at her daughter's party the next Saturday afternoon!

I explained that she would have to talk to my parents first. She came over that night, and the deal was on. I had my first job! Well, the kids at the party really liked my act. One of the mothers helping out decided

she wanted me to come to *her* kid's party, which was coming up in two weeks.

Now it's October, and I'm entertaining at about two parties a week. Some jobs come from the posters and my ad in the paper. And some come through Bradford! He tells everyone he knows about "my brother the juggler."

My mother said one of the kids she tutors would love a juggling octopus at his birthday party in January. And the other day, Officer Double-chin Simmons called to ask if I could perform at a party for the Policemen's Benevolent Association!

Since my juggling career started, I haven't felt so shy or stuck for things to say to people. It seems as if everyone wants to know how I got started juggling.

It's fun to walk home with Gramps and talk about the things that happen at parties. I'm still volunteering at the orphanage with him too, even though my two "punishment months" are up. I'm never sitting around with nothing to do anymore.

And I'm making money! By the end of September, I had bought myself ten new Fantastic Zippo comic books, new orange sneakers for my costume, stage makeup and the red plastic robot that says "Beep bop boop." (At least it used to say "Beep bop boop." My mother was right—it broke the first time I played with it.)

If business stays good, I'm planning to buy Gary a soccer ball (running after the ball should help him

lose weight) and new eyeglasses for Louise, with frames she likes.

I have big plans to become an even better juggler. I've started practicing with hoops and clubs, besides oranges and tennis balls. And some day, I hope to juggle five raw eggs!

I'm not famous throughout Cambridge yet, but our school paper did have an article about me. Bradford thinks I'm a real celebrity. And once in a while, some kid who went to a birthday party where I performed stops me in the street and says, "I know you! You're Chooch the Orange Octopus!" I don't mind that at all.

CORDUROY
Writes a Letter

A Viking Easy-to-Read

Story by **Alison Inches**

Illustrations by **Allan Eitzen**

Based on the characters created by
Don Freeman

VIKING

VIKING
Published by the Penguin Group
Penguin Putnam Books for Young Readers,
345 Hudson Street, New York, New York 10014, U.S.A.
Penguin Books Ltd, 80 Strand, London WC2R 0RL, England
Penguin Books Australia Ltd, Ringwood, Victoria, Australia
Penguin Books Canada Ltd, 10 Alcorn Avenue, Toronto, Ontario, Canada M4V 3B2
Penguin Books (N.Z.) Ltd, 182-190 Wairau Road, Auckland 10, New Zealand

Penguin Books Ltd, Registered Offices: Harmondsworth, Middlesex, England

First published in 2002 by Viking,
a division of Penguin Putnam Books for Young Readers.

1 3 5 7 9 10 8 6 4 2

Copyright © Penguin Putnam Inc., 2002
Text by Alison Inches
Illustrations by Allan Eitzen
All rights reserved

LIBRARY OF CONGRESS CATALOGING-IN-PUBLICATION DATA
Inches, Alison.
Corduroy writes a letter / by Alison Inches ; illustrated by Allan Eitzen;
p. cm.
Based on a character created by Don Freeman.
Summary: Corduroy shows Lisa that writing letters to express
your opinion can make a difference.
ISBN 0-670-03548-3
[1. Letter writing—Fiction. 2. Letters—Fiction. 3. Teddy
bears—Fiction.] I. Eitzen, Allan, ill. II. Freeman, Don, 1908-1978.
III. Title.
PZ7.I355 Cmk 2002
[E]—dc21
2002006154

Viking ® and Easy-to-Read ® are registered trademarks of Penguin Putnam Inc.

Printed in Hong Kong
Set in Bookman

Reading Level 1.8

CORDUROY
Writes a Letter

Lisa took a big bite of her cookie.

"*Hmmm*," she said.

"Something's different. I know what it is.

It doesn't have enough sprinkles!"

"Why don't you write the bakery a letter?"

said her mother.

"Tell them the cookies need

more sprinkles."

"Good idea!" said Lisa.

She got out a pen

and a pad of paper.

She stared at the pad.

The clock went

Tick tick.

Tick tick.

After a while, she said,

"What's the use, Corduroy?

The bakery owner will not listen to me.

I'm just a little girl."

She put down her pen and left.

Maybe I can write a letter, thought Corduroy.

He wrote:

Dear Mr. Bakery Owner:

We love your cookies.

We buy them every Saturday.

Today there were fewer sprinkles.

We thought you should know.

Yours sincerely,

Corduroy

Corduroy put the letter in an envelope
and mailed it.

The next Saturday, Lisa and Corduroy
picked up the cookies.

"Look, Corduroy!" said Lisa.

"The cookies have more sprinkles!"

"That's right!" said the owner.

"Someone sent me a letter."

That night, Lisa and her mother went

to the movies.

Corduroy went, too.

"Hey, look at the sign!" said Lisa.

"The lights are out on two of the letters.

The sign says MOVIE EATER.

It should say MOVIE THEATER."

Lisa and her mother laughed.

"Why don't you write the owner a letter?"

said her mother.

"Maybe I will," said Lisa.

After the movie, Lisa got a pen and a pad of paper.

"What should I write, Corduroy?" said Lisa.

She thought and thought.

Soon Lisa began to feel sleepy.

"It's no use," said Lisa.

"The movie theater owner is too important.

He will not read a letter from me."

She went to bed.

But Corduroy was not ready for bed.

I can write a letter, thought Corduroy.

Corduroy got the pen and pad.

He sat under the night-light and wrote:

Dear Mr. Movie Theater Owner:

Last night, we went to your theater.

We noticed your sign.

Two of your lights are out.

Yours truly,

Corduroy

On Thursday, Lisa and her mother
walked past the movie theater.

THEATER

Lisa looked at the sign.

"It's all fixed!" she said.

"It *is* fixed," said a man sweeping.
"Someone wrote me a letter.
It said two of my lights were out,
so I fixed them."

"That's neat," said Lisa.

"The next time I have something to say,

I'm going to write a letter."

Every day, Lisa listened to music on the radio.

Corduroy listened, too.

"I love this new radio station," said Lisa.

"But I wish they would play 'Teddy Bear Bop.'

That's my favorite song.

"I should write the station

and ask them to play it," said Lisa.

Great idea! thought Corduroy.

Lisa got her pen and pad.

She wrote:

Dear WROC:

I listen to your station every day.

I wish you would play "Teddy Bear Bop."

It's my favorite song.

It's my bear Corduroy's favorite song, too.

Thanks for being the best station ever.

Yours truly,

Lisa

Lisa put the letter into an envelope

and mailed it.

The following week,

Lisa had the radio on.

The deejay said,

"This next song is for Corduroy

from Lisa."

Then "Teddy Bear Bop" began to play.

Lisa and Corduroy danced around

the room.

"Wow!" said Lisa.

"They're playing our song!"

See, thought Corduroy.

It pays to write letters!